MW00896801

The author would like to thank those family members, friends and colleagues who have given their encouragement and support for this project.

A special thanks goes to Roberto Gonzalez roberto@rogolart.com | www.rogolart.ca for his wonderful creativity and expertise in illustrating and formatting this book.

The Honeybee That Learned To Dance

Text copyright © 2014 by Sharon Clark
Illustrations copyright © 2014 by Roberto Gonzalez
All rights reserved. No part of this book may be reproduced in any form or by electronic or mechanical means – except for brief quotations for use in articles or reviews - without permission in writing from the publisher.

For information about permission to reproduce selections from this book, contact Sharon Clark at sharon.clark@me.com

Printed in the USA

ISBN: 978-1496060402

The Honeybee That Learned To Dance

By Sharon Clark

Illustrated by Roberto Gonzalez

*H*ummy, the honeybee, awoke to buzzing vibrations. She realized immediately that today was special because her sisters had gathered in a circle around her.
One approached her with a gift of food.
Another began cleaning Hummy's wings.
The rest simply wagged their bottoms with joy.
Hummy had seen this ritual many times before.
It meant that today, she would be given the most important duty of all.

Today she would become a forager.

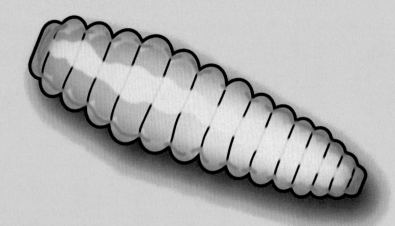

A *few weeks ago, Hummy had hatched from an egg
laid by the queen bee inside of a honeycomb cell.
She had been a worm-like larva, whose only job was
to eat and grow bigger.
Eventually, she spun a silk cocoon around herself and
became a pupa.
At this stage in her life she rested quietly while great
changes occurred to her form.
She developed eyes, antennae, wings and legs.
Her whole body changed shape until she looked just
like an adult honeybee.
She crawled out of her cocoon and began her new
life inside of the hive.*

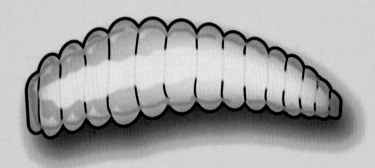

At first she had been too small and her wings had been too weak for her to fly.
So she had been given housekeeping chores.
She cleaned her cell and others around it.
After a while, she was allowed to feed other bees and other larvae.
When she was big enough, she was finally given the honor of bringing food to the queen bee.
Every day she grew bigger and stronger.
She learned how to build new honeycomb cells for the storage of nectar.
Her last duty had been very important.
She had learned how to guard and protect the entrance to the hive.

Now, Hummy savored the food that had been given to her. She needed plenty of nourishment before she explored the world outside of her hive.
She nibbled at the pollen. It would provide protein to strengthen her wing muscles. As she ate, she glanced out of the hive at the sky beyond.

It was a hot and sunny day.
She could sense vibrations from birds singing in the distance. The leaves on the trees were moving gently in the light breeze.
Today she must enter this strange new world. As of this day forward, her new duties would be to leave the security and safety of the hive to search for food. She was very excited, but she was also quite afraid. What new and scary things might she encounter in this strange world? What if she couldn't find food to bring back to the others? What would happen if she got lost and couldn't find her way home? Whatever would she do?

Hummy ate the pollen slowly. She wasn't sure she was ready to become a forager. Even if she found food and could find her way home, would she remember how to dance? A few days ago, she had carefully observed the rituals that occurred when a forager returned. Other foragers within the hive would form a circle around the returning bee and carefully watch her dance.

Sometimes, if the forager had only been gone a short while, she would perform a simple round dance.

The other bees would know immediately that food was very near. They would fly off excitedly, moving in ever widening circles around the hive until the source of food was found. At other times, if the forager had been gone a long time, she would do a more complicated waggle dance. The others needed to watch her closely, for the way she danced would tell them how far away the source of food was and it's direction. Hummy was pretty sure that she remembered how to do the round dance.

But could she remember the more complex waggle dance? She hoped so. She desperately wanted to be the best forager she could possibly be.

As Hummy finished the last of her pollen, she groomed the crumbs off her slender legs.
The bees that had attended to her began to move away. One took the lead and guided Hummy to the entrance to the hive. The others followed, wagging their behinds encouragingly.
The lead bee pointed to the sun, reminding Hummy to always be mindful of its position. Hummy looked out of the hive at the great expanse of land and sky.
Her little heart was pounding and she hesitated for just a moment. Then, when she glanced back at the others eagerly awaiting her flight, she realized that she didn't want to let them down. She took a deep breath, mustered all of her strength and courage, then forced her wings into a powerful downstroke.

To her astonishment, she was suddenly airborne. Excitedly, she experimented with the positioning and beat of her wings. Quickly, she mastered how to fly higher or faster. And in another short time, she also learned how to change direction. Joyously, she circled high above her hive, dipping and turning and rising again.

Hummy was so thrilled with her new abilities that she almost forgot why she was there. As she rose up into the sky, she spotted the sun and suddenly remembered what she had to do. She noted the sun's position relative to the hive, then flew off in a westerly direction.

The sky was a brilliant blue, with only the odd fluffy cloud in sight. The trees below her were various shades of green. These were colors she had never seen before. Below were two creatures that were very different from her. One was far larger than Hummy. The other was smaller than the first, but still huge in Hummy's eyes. The smaller creature had wings, but was not a honeybee. Hummy knew this because it was still much larger than her and it only had two legs. When it took flight, Hummy watched in wonder as it easily moved from ground to tree. The larger creature was very strange. It didn't have wings or six legs like Hummy. And it seemed to be putting something yellow into the ground.

Hummy swooped down to take a closer look at the bright yellow object. Her antennae picked up a sweet, floral fragrance mixed with nectar. Perhaps this was a good spot to collect nectar to bring back to the hive. But, just as she was about to land on one of the petals, the large creature flung one of its parts at her. Hummy quickly changed direction and just missed being hit. Maybe this wasn't the best place to look for nectar after all.

*S*o, Hummy rose high in the sky once again. She looked in all directions at the landscape. To one side of her was a structure with something attached that flapped in the wind.

But further away was a large green field with many golden patches inside of it. No large, scary creatures were anywhere in sight.

She decided to take a closer look. As she circled above the golden patch, her antennae again sensed a sweet fragrance. No danger seemed to be near, so she landed on a petal of one of the golden blossoms.

COMMUNITY SCHOOL

Her eyes were equipped with special vision that allowed her to see precisely where the nectar was within the flower. So she uncoiled a long drinking part, much like a straw, and inserted it into the nectar. She drank heartily, storing it in her honeysac stomach. Pollen accumulated on her body as she moved within the flower, so she used the brushes of her front and middle legs to store it in her pollen baskets on her hind legs.

*O*nce one flower was emptied of its nectar, Hummy moved to the next. She worked busily gathering food for her hive until both her honeysac stomach and her pollen baskets were full. Now it was time to return home. Briefly, she sat on one of the petals and looked up into the sky. Over an hour had passed since she left her hive. The sun's position had changed. She knew that she would have to adjust her direction of flight relative to the sun. Otherwise, she would get terribly lost! Could she make the right decision? Again, she felt afraid. If she made a mistake, she might never find her way home!

Hummy took a deep breath, looked at the position of the sun and made a decision. She flew on a path that she hoped would lead her home. With her heavy load, her wings had to work much harder to lift her up into the air. But the pollen she had eaten before her flight had strengthened them.
She rose higher and higher into the blue sky.

*A*s she picked up speed, she began to worry.
Nothing looked familiar. Oh, dear, was she lost?
What would she do if she couldn't find her hive?
Hummy's little heart began to pound. But then, off to
the right, something caught her attention. It was that
structure with the flapping thing. She headed towards
it and began to recognize the landscape beneath her.
Over familiar fields and trees she went. When she saw
the large creature still busy at it's activities, she felt a
sense of relief. She was on the right path.

*Suddenly, Hummy recognized a familiar scent.
She had been born and raised in that scent.
It was her home. Excitedly she flew in its direction
until she saw it in the distance.
Her hive - her beautiful hive! Some of her sisters
were guarding the entrance and fanning their wings
to disperse the hive's scent. Hummy was overjoyed.*

The guard bees wagged their bottoms in greeting as she approached the hive.
But they cautiously touched her all over with their antennae to make sure her scent matched that of the hive. When they were satisfied that she was one of their sisters, they quickly let her pass.

As she moved inside, another excited group of bees surrounded her. She transferred her nectar into the mouths of these waiting worker bees.

Each then hurried off to store it in special cells within the honeycomb. Hummy headed off in another direction. She busily emptied her pollen baskets into another group of cells. When this task was finished, Hummy felt satisfied and proud of what she had accomplished. She had successfully foraged for food and found her way home.

*B*ut to be one of the most valuable foragers in the hive, Hummy still needed to pass one more test. She needed to dance to tell other foragers where to find this food. Would she remember how to dance? Other foragers eagerly formed a circle around her. Hummy had travelled quite a distance before she found the food that she brought back. So she knew that it would be necessary to perform the more complicated waggle dance. She looked at the other bees eagerly awaiting her movements.
Then she took a deep breath and began to dance.

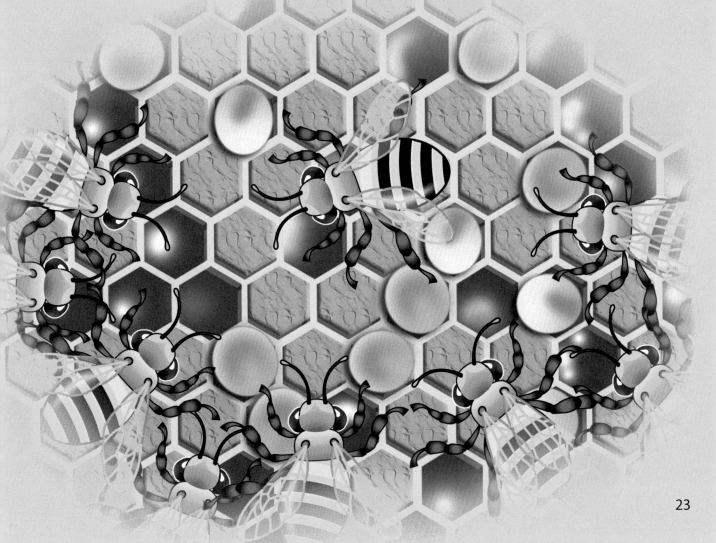

Slowly she danced in a half circle in the honeycomb, and suddenly ran at an angle up and to the right. This angle told the others that they needed to travel in a direction that was to the right of the sun. During her run, she also occasionally wagged her abdomen. The number of waggles that she did, told the others how far away the food would be found. In one second, she did four waggles that told them the food was about 1000 yards away. She followed this display by dancing in a half circle in the opposite direction, and finally returned to her starting point. Then she repeated the waggle dance.

The others also touched her with their antennae so they could smell the kinds of flowers that she had visited. Suddenly, one by one, they began to fly off. After the last forager left, Hummy felt very tired. She had to wait to see if the others could find her food.

In the meantime she would take a much-deserved rest.

As Hummy sat quietly in the corner of the honeycomb, a worker rushed up to her with a gift of nectar. Another followed with a gift of pollen. Hummy welcomed the nourishment and felt her strength returning as she ate.

After what seemed like a very long while, Hummy's antennae detected vibrations.
At first these vibrations were weak, but they were becoming stronger and stronger. Hummy realized that they were coming from the foragers who were return-ing. Had they found her food? Would she be considered a valuable forager for the hive? Suddenly, workers all around her were becoming very excited.

*T*he foragers were loaded with food. The hive began
to buzz with activity. Each forager emptied her supply,
afterwards approaching Hummy.
One by one they formed a circle around her.
Then each returning forager used her antennae to
stroke Hummy's wings.

This was the highest honor of all.
Hummy was bursting with pride.
She had overcome her fears and bravely tested her abilities. She had reached her full potential.
She had become a successful forager and she had also learned to dance.

31705570R00020

Made in the USA
San Bernardino, CA
17 March 2016